Printed in the U.S.A.

ISBN 0-7172-8288-0

JIM HENSON'S MUPPETS

IN

New in Town

A Book About Shyness

By Ellen Weiss • Illustrated by Joel Schick

GROLIER

Bean Bunny sat on the back of the moving van, looking out at his new neighborhood. He was wishing he hadn't moved at all.

"Look, Bean," said his mother. "There are two kids right down the block. Why don't you go say hi?"

"Um—I don't think so," said Bean.

"Too shy?" said his mother.

"Too shy," said Bean.

Fozzie and Kermit were playing catch in Kermit's yard. "Hey. It's a new kid!" said Kermit.

"Should we go say hello?" asked Fozzie.

"Okay," said Kermit. "Maybe he'll want to play with us."

But when Bean saw Fozzie and Kermit
coming, he jumped down from the back of the
truck and ran into his house.

"I guess he's not too friendly," said Kermit.

"Guess not," said Fozzie.

They didn't know that Bean was just having
a shyness attack.

Inside the house, Bean was feeling scared. *What if they don't like me?* he thought. *In my old neighborhood, everybody liked me, but that's because they knew me.*

He looked out the window at the two kids. *I'm probably really different from them,* he thought. *They look like they're such good friends. Why would they want to make friends with me?*

The next day, Bean was at the supermarket with his mother. There, next to the cottage cheese, was Piggy. When she saw Bean, she smiled at him.

Oh, no! thought Bean. *What'll I do?* So he ducked behind his mother until Piggy had gone.

That Monday was Bean's first day at school. Piggy and Skeeter saw him standing in the schoolyard before the bell rang.

"Who's the new kid?" asked Skeeter.

"I don't know," said Piggy. "But I don't think he's very friendly."

For weeks, every day was the same. Bean spoke to no one and played with no one. He just stayed in his room every day after school.

"I don't understand it," said his mother one afternoon. "You were never shy in our old neighborhood. In fact, you were, well, sort of loud."

"I knew everybody there," said Bean.

One cold, damp day in October, Bean was walking home alone from school. As usual, he took the short way, cutting across the park. And as usual, he was glad nobody was around; that meant he wouldn't have to try to talk to anybody.

The sky got darker. Bean felt a drop of rain on his nose, then another.

Suddenly, there was a flash of lightning, and then, a moment later, a rumble of thunder.

Uh-oh, thought Bean. He walked faster.

The rain started coming down harder. There was a bright crack of lightning and a loud clap of thunder soon after.

Bean looked around him. He knew it wasn't safe to be out in the open in a lightning storm. He had to find shelter. But where could he go?

Aha! He could stay in the shed where all the baseball equipment was stored.

Bean made a run for it.

Bean sprinted the last few steps to the shed, yanked open the door, and ran inside.

Whew! He was safe. The rain pounded on the roof, and a thunderclap sounded.

As Bean's eyes began adjusting to the dark, he could make out a rack full of bats, a scoreboard, and a stack of bases.

Suddenly, he noticed two pairs of eyes staring out at him.

"Hello?" said a voice. "Who's there?"

"B-b-b-bean Bunny, the new kid," answered Bean nervously. "Who are you?"

Bean heard two sighs of relief. "Kermit and Fozzie," said the voice, which belonged to Kermit.

"Stay here and keep dry with us," added Fozzie.

"Fozzie was just telling me a werewolf joke," said Kermit.

"Yeah," said Fozzie. "Which side of a werewolf has the most fur?"

"I—I don't know," said Bean shyly.

"The outside!" laughed Fozzie.

Kermit laughed, too, and so did Bean.

"Do you know any jokes?" Fozzie asked Bean.

Bean thought about it. "Yup," he said. "What's worse than finding a worm in your apple?"

"What?" said Kermit.

"Finding half a worm," said Bean.

"Yuck! Gross!" said Kermit. He and Fozzie laughed and laughed.

For a while after that, Bean, Kermit, and
Fozzie listened to the rain beating on the roof.

"Let's sing a song," said Kermit finally. So
they sang "On Top of Spaghetti." Then they
sang six more songs.

"Wow," said Bean. "You guys know the same
songs I do."

Next, Bean, Kermit, and Fozzie named every baseball record they could think of. Then they told ghost stories.

"Look," said Fozzie, pointing out the window. "The sun's coming out!"

The rain had stopped pounding on the roof, too.

"Let's go!" said Kermit. "Our parents are probably worried about us."

Bean, Kermit, and Fozzie gathered up their books. "Hey, I'm glad we all ended up in here together," said Bean.

"Me, too," said Fozzie.

"This was the most fun I've ever had during a thunderstorm!" Kermit added.

"You know," Bean admitted as they walked home, "when I first moved here, I was really shy. You seemed so different from my old friends. But you're really a lot like them."

"What were they like?" Kermit asked.

Bean thought for a moment. "Nice," he finally said.

The next day, Kermit and Fozzie intro-
duced Bean to Piggy and Gonzo and all their
other friends. And from that day on, Bean
Bunny, the shy new kid, was just plain Bean
Bunny, part of the gang.

Let's Talk About Shyness

When Bean Bunny moved to town, he had a lot of trouble making friends because he was feeling shy. But when he spent some time with Kermit and Fozzie, they had a lot of fun together. That made Bean feel more comfortable. He was able to stop feeling so shy and start making friends.

Here are some questions about shyness for you to think about:

Do you feel shy when you're doing something for the first time, like starting in a new school or meeting some new people?

How could you help another person who is feeling shy?